D1367214

Superfast Cars™

Porsche

Rebecca Hawley

PowerKiDS
press.
New York

Published in 2007 by The Rosen Publishing Group, Inc.
29 East 21st Street, New York, NY 10010

First Edition

Editor: Joanne Randolph
Book Design: Ginny Chu
Book Layout: Kate Laczynski
Photo Researcher: Sam Cha

Photo Credits: All Photos © Getty Images.

Library of Congress Cataloging-in-Publication Data

Hawley, Rebecca.
   Porsche / Rebecca Hawley. — 1st. ed.
      p. cm. — (Superfast cars)
   Includes index.
   ISBN-13: 978-1-4042-3641-7 (library binding)
   ISBN-10: 1-4042-3641-4 (library binding)
   1. Porsche automobiles—Juvenile literature. I. Title.
   TL215.P75H375 2007
   629.222'2—dc22
                                        2006021017

Manufactured in the United States of America

Contents

Here a Porsche 911 races a Russian jet. Porsche is known for making fast cars.

What Is a Fast Car?

Imagine you could go from standing still to moving at 60 miles per hour (97 km/h) in just a few seconds. If you are sitting inside a fast car, this is possible. Fast cars are on the cutting edge of **technology** and **design**. They are beautiful and powerful. They are built to move quickly. They are also built to hug corners and hang onto the road. Who wouldn't want to know more about these wonderful machines?

Here is a Porsche 356, now more than 50 years old. Porsche made 50 356s in all.

The History of Porsche

If you are interested in fast cars, then you know the name Porsche. Ferry Porsche started the Porsche company. He based many of the design ideas on those of his father, Ferdinand, who was an **engineer**. Porsche made its first sports car in 1948.

In 1950, Porsche became an **independent** factory in Germany. Today it sells cars to people around the world. Porsche feels that it makes more than just cars. Porsche is also a way of life.

This is the Porsche factory and testing center in Leipzig. The factory has 800 workers.

Where It All Happens

You might wonder how Porsche makes such cool, fast cars. It takes the best designers and top technology. Porsche's first factory could not produce enough cars. So the company built a new factory in Leipzig, Germany. The factory is **state-of-the-art**. Porsche uses the factory to make the Cayenne and the Carrera GT, two of its newest **models**. It has a test track and a track where safe-driving classes are offered to Porsche owners.

To be sure its cars will stand the test of time, Porsche does all sorts of tests. Workers open and close the side windows of the cars 40,000 times and shut the doors 100,000 times.

The Test of Time

It takes a lot of hard work to make fast cars as well as Porsche does. Porsche tests everything on its cars. Workers check to see how fast the car can go. They make sure that the car will work smoothly in any kind of weather and on even the bumpiest roads.

What is the result of all this testing? Nearly three-quarters of all the Porsches ever built are still driven. These cars really last!

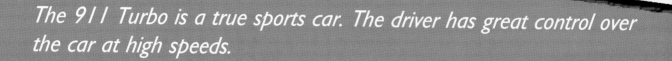

The 911 Turbo is a true sports car. The driver has great control over the car at high speeds.

Meet the 911 Turbo

The first 911 model came out in 1964. The car helped **define** Porsche's look and feel. It also defined what a sports car should be for the world. The 911 has been made in many forms since 1964. The latest is the 911 Turbo. The Turbo is truly a fast car. It has a top **speed** of 193 miles per hour (311 km/h). It can reach 60 miles per hour (97 km/h) in less than 4 seconds.

This Carrera GT is being tested on the track at Leipzig. People can have the car hand made to fit their needs exactly.

14

Meet the Carrera GT

In 2004, Porsche gave us the Carrera GT. It is no surprise that this car was based on Porsche's race cars. It has a top speed of 205 miles per hour (330 km/h). That is a superfast car! The car also handles well. It rounds corners smoothly and easily. It holds tightly to the road, even at the highest speeds.

This car goes beyond the common sports car. It is a supercar.

The Cayman's body shape helps air move smoothly over the car. This means that air will not slow the car down too much.

Cayman S

Meet the Cayman S

In 2006, Porsche presented the Cayman S. This car is based on Porsche's **classic** Boxster. Though the Cayman S is not as fast as the Turbo or the Carrera GT, it is still a fast car. It moves quickly and smoothly. The driver has great control over the car, even at high speeds. The Cayman S reaches top speeds of 171 miles per hour (275 km/h) and can hit 60 miles per hour (97 km/h) in 5 seconds.

Porsche cars are raced around the world. This car is racing on a track in Florida.

From the Start

Since it first began making cars, Porsche has made race cars. It has long made race cars that win, too. In the past 50 or so years, Porsche has won over 23,000 races. It is no wonder that the people at Porsche know so much about making cars that go superfast.

They have their own drivers who race worldwide. Many of the people who own their cars race them in **amateur** races, too.

You can see how alike this race car is to the cars Porsche sells for use on the road. Porsche applies the cutting-edge technology needed for winning races to building great fast cars.

From the Track to the Road

Until 1962, Porsche made and raced cars for **long-distance** races, and it also made **Formula 1** cars, such as the 804 Formel 1. Since 1962, Porsche has spent most of its time making cars for long-distance races, though. The company believes making and racing these cars helps it build cars for the road as well. It can use what it learns in the races to make better sports cars.

What Lies Ahead?

Porsche has been making cars for more than 50 years. It is sure to be wowing people with its cars for many years to come, too. Right now Porsche has plans to build a four-door, four-seat sports car called the Panamera. This car will come out in 2009.

People who love fast cars will look forward to whatever Porsche does next. It is sure to be something beautiful. It is also sure to be something fast.

Glossary

amateur (A-muh-tur) Someone who does something because they like it. They do not get paid for it.

classic (KLA-sik) Standing the test of time and being a common example of something.

define (dih-FYN) To give meaning to something.

design (dih-ZYN) The plan or the form of something.

engineer (en-juh-NEER) A master at planning and building engines, machines, roads, and bridges.

Formula 1 (FOR-myuh-luh WUN) A kind of car used in racing. It has one seat and its wheels are on the outside of the car's body.

independent (in-dih-PEN-dent) Free from the control of others.

long-distance (long-DIS-tens) Something that is far away or a long way.

models (MAH-dulz) Kinds of cars.

speed (SPEED) How quickly something moves.

state-of-the-art (STAYT-uv-thee-art) At the top of technology.

technology (tek-NAH-luh-jee) The way that people do something using tools and the tools that they use.

Index

Web Sites

Due to the changing nature of Internet links, PowerKids Press has developed an online list of Web sites related to the subject of this book. This site is updated regularly. Please use this link to access the list:
www.powerkidslinks.com/sfc/porsche/